MORE STORIES FOR THE VERY YOUNG

Selected and edited by
SALLY GRINDLEY

Illustrated by
TONI GOFFE

Kingfisher Books

Kingfisher Books, Grisewood & Dempsey Ltd,
Elsley House, 24-30 Great Titchfield Street,
London W1P 7AD

First published in 1992 by Kingfisher Books
2 4 6 8 10 9 7 5 3 1

The material in this book was previously published
by Kingfisher Books in *Stories for the Very Young* (1989)

BRITISH LIBRARY CATALOGUING IN PUBLICATION DATA
A catalogue record for this book is available from the British Library

Printed in Hong Kong

For permission to reproduce copyright material, acknowledgement
and thanks are due to the following:
Victor Gollancz Ltd on the author's behalf for "Because of
Figs" by Ann Cameron from *The Julian Stories* and Jonathan
Cape Ltd on the author's behalf for "The Little Boy's Secret"
by David L. Harrison from *The Book of Giant Stories*
illustrated by Philippe Fix.

CONTENTS

IT'S A GOOD HONEST NAME

Dick King-Smith

Mr and Mrs Doddipoll's first baby was a boy. He was a very long baby.

"What shall we call him?" said Mr Doddipoll.

"John," said Mrs Doddipoll. "It's a good honest name."

A year later, Mrs Doddipoll had a second baby. It was another boy.

"What shall we call him?" said Mr Doddipoll.

"John," said Mrs Doddipoll. "It's a good honest name."

The father looked a bit worried. "We've got one John," he said.

"We can easily tell them apart," said the mother. "This one's not going to be tall like his brother. He's going to be short."

So they called the new baby Short John and his elder brother Long John.

Another year passed, and another baby was born, a little brother for Long John and Short John.

"Another John, I suppose?" said Mr Doddipoll.

"Naturally," said Mrs Doddipoll. This baby was a skinny little chap, so of course he was called Thin John.

And guess what – after another year along came a fourth brother who was very tubby. By now the father had given up asking silly questions about what to call a new baby. He just took one look at the child and said, "Fat John?"

"Of course," said the mother. "Bring the others to see him."

Thin John who was one year old took a look and said, "Wah!"

Short John, who was two, said, "Bay-bee!"

And Long John, who was three and already very tall, said, "John!"

"Fat John," said his parents.

"Look!" said Long John to Short John and Thin John, pointing into the cradle. "Look! Fat John!"

"Bay-bee!" said Short John.

"Wah!" said Thin John.

One day when the four Johns were another year older, they went for a walk together. Short John (who was strong) gave Thin John (who was light) a piggyback. This made them together as tall as Long John (who was carrying Fat John in his arms). It was a lovely day.

When they finally got back home again, their father was standing in the doorway looking out for them.

"Hello, Johns," said Mr Doddipoll. "I've got a surprise for you. Guess what?"

Long John put Fat John down on the ground.

"Mother's had another baby?" he said.

Short John lifted Thin John off his shoulders.

"'Nother John?" he said.

"Bay-bee," said Thin John.

"Wah!" said Fat John.

"Yes, there's another baby," said Mr Doddipoll. "But we're not going to call this one John."

"You're not going to call it John, father?" said Long John in an unhappy voice. "It's a good honest name."

The other three boys looked miserable.

"No more Johns?" said Short John sadly.

"Poor b-bay-bee!" moaned Thin John.

And as for Fat John, he burst into floods of tears.

"Wah! Wah! Wah!" he yelled.

Mr Doddipoll put his arms around the four Johns and when Fat John had stopped yelling he said, "There's a good reason, you see, why we're not going to call this one John. Because it's a girl. Come and see her."

"Hello, Johns," said Mrs Doddipoll. "What do you think of your new baby sister?"

The four Johns looked at the baby girl, but they did not answer, except for Fat John, who said, "Wah!" very softly, under his breath.

"We're going to call her Janet," said Mrs Doddipoll.

But the funny thing is that the four John Doddipolls never did call her by her real name. They grew up to be men, and they lived to be old men, and they looked after their only sister well.

But neither Long John nor Short John nor Thin John nor Fat John ever called her Janet.

They called her Girl John. After all, it's a good honest name.

SALLY'S WOOLLY ELEPHANT

Adèle Geras

Sally's woolly elephant, dressed in his
striped woolly scarf, thought it was a
lovely afternoon for a walk.

All the tree-trunks and branches were frosty and glittering in the sun, the roofs were white and shining, the leaves and grass were sprinkled with icy powder.

"How pretty it looks," thought Sally's woolly elephant, "and how pleasant it is to feel warm. It's good to be a woolly elephant on a cold afternoon."

At that moment, he saw a robin sitting on a gate.

"Hello, robin," he said. "Splendid day, isn't it?"

"I suppose it looks splendid," agreed the robin, "but it's chilly all the same. Could I ride on your back as far as the park? My feet are very cold."

"I'm afraid I can't let you do that," said Sally's woolly elephant. "Your feet are dirty and I don't want mud on my woolly back. Hope you don't mind. Goodbye."

And the woolly elephant shuffled off through the crisp leaves.

"Hello, woolly elephant," cried the pigeons outside the library. "Chilly, isn't it? Could we ride on your warm back as far as the bakery? The baker throws out a lot of crumbs on Tuesdays and it's a long way in this weather."

"I'd like to take you," said the woolly elephant, "but there are a lot of you and you'd make my back very dirty, so I must say no, I'm afraid. Bye-bye."

And away he slid on the frozen puddles.

"Hello, woolly elephant," said the brown kitten who was sitting on the step outside the butcher's shop. "You look warm and cosy. I like your stripey scarf. Would you lend it to me while I wait here? I'll have to wait a long time before I get any scraps, you know, and walking will keep you warm."

"I'm sorry, kitten," said Sally's woolly elephant, "but it's my very own *special* scarf, and I shouldn't like to part with it. Goodbye."

And he slipped along the slippery pavement.

At last the woolly elephant reached the park. He walked down the grey paths, looked at the frozen pink roses left over from the summer, smiled at the babies bundled into their warm prams, waved his trunk at the old men in black hats sitting on the benches, and made his way to the swings.

"Isn't it cold, woolly elephant?" shouted the children as he swung himself through the air.

"Not if you're a woolly elephant," he replied, and he sang this little song as the swing went up and down:

"When the weather's cold and icy
Being woolly's very nicey;
Being chilly's very silly
But it's bully to be woolly!"

Sally's elephant was having such fun that he forgot the time. The sun went down, the lamps were already glowing in the street outside the park.

"Gosh, it's late," said the woolly elephant. "I must go home or Sally will be worried."

Just then the mist came down, muffling the trees, hiding the houses, blanketing the lights. The woolly elephant could see the tip of his trunk and that was all.

"How shall I ever get home?" he thought. "I can't see the way. I'll miss my supper. I'll have to stay out all night with no one to talk to. Whatever shall I do?"

And he began to cry.

"Don't cry, woolly elephant," said a small voice down near his feet. "It's me, the kitten from the butcher's shop. I'll help you to find your way home. I was chasing a bird and the mist came down just before I caught it."

The kitten jumped onto the woolly elephant's back and guided him to the street. Cats can see in the dark. When they came to the butcher's shop, the kitten jumped off.

"There you are, woolly elephant. Just follow the street lights and you'll soon be home."

"Thank you," said the woolly elephant. "I'm sorry I didn't lend you my scarf. You may borrow it now if you're cold."

"You keep it for the moment," said the kitten, "but I'd love to wear it for a while tomorrow."

"You shall have it for as long as you like," said Sally's woolly elephant, and he plodded away into the mist.

"It must be awfully late," he thought. "There's no one about. I think I'm a bit frightened and I know I'm lonely."

Suddenly he heard a rush of wings and a whole flock of pigeons settled on his back. "Don't be frightened," they cooed. "We'll sing to you and cheer you up."

They sat on the elephant's back, singing happy songs into his woolly ears until he came to the traffic lights.

"I'll take you for a ride again tomorrow," he told them as they flew off. "I'm sorry I didn't take you when you asked. I hope you had lots of crumbs to eat. Goodnight."

Sally's woolly elephant was nearly home now, but the mist was so thick that he could not read the names of the roads.

"Oh dear," he sighed. "Is it this one or the next one? I'll never find it. What shall I do?"

"Come with me," said the robin, settling on the elephant's trunk. "I'll show you the road and the house."

He flew along just in front of the woolly elephant, and led him right to the back door of Sally's house. Yellow light was pouring out of the kitchen window, and Sally was eating hot buttered toast at the table.

"Thank you so much, robin," said the elephant. "I'm sorry I didn't take you to the park today. Shall we go there together tomorrow?"

"That would be delightful," said the robin. "Goodbye, woolly elephant."

And he disappeared into the branches of the pear tree in the garden next door.

The following day, Sally's woolly elephant took the robin on his back and set off for the park. When they reached the library, all the pigeons fluttered down, singing and jostling one another. Just outside the baker's shop they rose in a grey cloud from the elephant's back, and swooped down to eat the crumbs. At the butcher's shop, the woolly elephant stopped to lend the kitten his scarf.

When they reached the park, the robin and the woolly elephant had a wonderful time on the swings. And they went home early together, while it was still light.

THE CLETTERKIN

Jenny Koralek

One morning after breakfast, Leggie Meggie ran into the garden to play with her new, yellow, very small, bouncy ball. And after one bounce she lost it. She rushed indoors calling, "Mum! Dad! Grannie! I've lost my new best ball!"

"I can't help you now," said Dad crossly. "I've lost my car keys. I will have to walk to work and I'll be very late."

"What we need in this house," said Grannie, "is a cletterkin."

But Dad didn't hear. He had gone, banging the door behind him.

"And I can't help you," said Mum. "I've lost my glasses. I've hunted high and low. I won't be able to read my book on the way to work and I'll be late too."

"What we need in this house," said Grannie, "is a cletterkin."

But Mum didn't hear. She had gone, banging the door behind her.

Leggie Meggie heard.

"What's a cletterkin?" she said.

Grannie looked up from her knitting. "A cletterkin finds things," she said. "And tidies what's untidy. A

16

cletterkin can see into all the little nooks and crannies,
indoors and out, where balls roll and car keys fall and
glasses lie. When I was a girl every house had a
cletterkin."

"What does a cletterkin look like?" asked Leggie
Meggie.

"I've never seen one myself," said Grannie. She
stopped to pick up a stitch from her knitting, "but . . ."

"But what?" said Leggie Meggie.

"Once I met a man who'd met a man who said . . . a
cletterkin has furry feet and leafy hair. He moves on feet
as soft as cats' paws. He can shoot up as tall as a tree and
shrink as small as a mouse. And because he can hunt

high and low, he can find high and low. I never saw the cletterkin in our house, but I know, I just know he was the one who always found my lost pocket-money penny and my brother's best blue marble."

"What was that noise?" said Leggie Meggie.

"What noise?" said Grannie.

"Soft on the floorboards like cats' paws," said Leggie Meggie.

"I heard nothing," yawned Grannie. "And now, oh dear, I've lost my knitting needle. I tell you, what we need in this house is a cletterkin."

She yawned again and began to nod off in her chair.

Leggie Meggie went back into the garden to look for her ball. She looked in the long grass. She looked under

the bushes. She fetched a stick and poked about in the stinging nettles. Where could it be?

"Perhaps it fell into one of the flowerpots," she said. She looked in three flowerpots. They were empty, except one which had a little bed of dry leaves and some snail shells full of raindrops. She was just about to put her hand into another flowerpot when a voice said:

"Didn't you know, long-leggedy, it's very rude to

scrabble about in people's houses? You've just unmade my bed and tipped over my cups."

There, by the flowerpot with the bed of dry leaves and the snail shells full of raindrops, was a little man with leafy hair and furry feet. He was sitting on Leggie Meggie's new, yellow, very small, bouncy ball.

"A cletterkin!" cried Leggie Meggie. "Just like Grannie said!"

"Not *a* cletterkin," said the little man. "*The* cletterkin, the *last* cletterkin."

"What happened to the others?" asked Leggie Meggie.

"They went away long ago to look for the rainbow's end," said the cletterkin.

"Oh dear," said Leggie Meggie.

"They'll never find it."

"I know," sighed the cletterkin.

"Don't be sad," said Leggie Meggie. "We need you in our house. Grannie says so every day because we're always losing things. Just in one morning I've lost my ball, Dad's lost his car keys, Mum's lost her glasses and Grannie's lost her knitting needle! Oh won't you be our cletterkin?"

"Well," said the cletterkin briskly, "you do sound like a very untidy family!" But he made that sound like something good. "If you've lost all those things since you got up this morning, who knows what you'll have lost by bedtime. I'd better get started straightaway."

So Leggie Meggie led the way into the house. She showed the cletterkin the cat-flap.

"You can always come in and out through there," she whispered, "when I'm not here to let you in. Because we will be secret about you, won't we?"

"Of course," said the cletterkin, "and anyway I have a little trick. I can make myself invisible if I want to."

"Go on then," said Leggie Meggie.

Suddenly the cletterkin had vanished, but Leggie Meggie heard his voice singing, "Cletter cletter, that's better." Then something scuttled through the newspaper lying like a tent on the floor, and there were Mum's glasses lying at Grannie's feet.

"Cletter cletter, that's better," came a voice from somewhere near the front door. "Car keys in an old wellie! There's enough work here for a hundred years."

There was a scurrying of feet as soft as cats' paws and there were Dad's keys lying at Grannie's feet.

"Cletter cletter, that's better," sang the invisible cletterkin, and Grannie's knitting needle seemed to heave itself up from a wide crack in the floorboards.

And there he was, sitting on top of Grannie's wool basket.

Just then the door banged and Leggie Meggie heard her mother calling.

"I must go now," she said.

"And I'm off to my house," said the cletterkin.

"I'll come out and play later," whispered Leggie Meggie, and the cletterkin shot out through the cat-flap.

When Mum and Dad saw all the lost things laid out at Grannie's feet, they were very pleased.

"Good girl, Leggie Meggie," said Dad.

"It wasn't me," said Leggie Meggie.

"Was it Grannie then?" They smiled at Grannie sleeping in her chair. "Dear Grannie, no wonder she's tired."

Then Grannie woke up. She saw her lost knitting needle neatly stuck into her wool. She saw Leggie Meggie holding her new, yellow, very small, bouncy ball. She saw the keys and Mum's glasses lying by her feet.

"Well," she said. "Perhaps there is a cletterkin about after all."

THE LITTLE BOY'S SECRET

David L. Harrison

One day a little boy left school early because he had a secret to tell his mother. He was in a hurry to get home, so he took a short cut through some woods where three terrible giants lived. He hadn't gone far before he met one of them standing in the path.

When the giant saw the little boy, he put his hands on his hips and roared, "What are you doing here, boy? Don't you know whose woods these are?"

"I'm on my way home," answered the little boy. "I have a secret to tell my mother."

That made the giant furious. "Secret?" he bellowed. "What secret?"

"I can't tell you," said the little

boy, "or it wouldn't be a secret any more."

"Then I'm taking you to our castle!" said the giant. Stooping down, he picked up the little boy and popped him into his shirt pocket.

Before long the first giant met a second giant who was twice as big, three times as ugly, and four times as fierce. "What's that in your pocket?" he asked the first giant.

"A boy," he answered. "Says he has a secret that he won't tell us."

When the second giant heard that, he laughed a wicked laugh. "Won't tell us, eh?" he chuckled. "Well, we'll just see about that! To the castle with him!"

The giants thumped on down the path. In a short time they came to a huge stone castle beside a muddy river.

At the door they met the third giant, who was five times bigger, six times uglier, and seven times fiercer than the second giant.

"What's that in your pocket?" he asked the first giant.

"A boy," he answered.

"A boy!" chuckled the third giant. He brought his huge eye close to the pocket and peered in.

"Says he has a secret he won't tell us," said the first giant.

When the third giant heard that, he laughed a terrible laugh. "Won't tell us, eh?" he asked. "Well, we'll just see about that! On the table with him!"

The first giant took the little boy from his pocket and set him on the kitchen table. Then all three giants gathered round and peered down at him.

The little boy looked at the first giant. He looked at the second giant. He looked at the third giant.

They were truly enormous and dreadful to behold.

"Well?" said the first giant.

"We're waiting," said the second giant.

"I'll count to three," said the third giant. "One .. two .."

The little boy sighed a big sigh.

"Oh, all right," he said. "I suppose I can tell you. But if I do, you must promise to let me go."

"We promise," answered the giants. But they all winked sly winks at one another and crossed their fingers behind their backs because they didn't really mean to let him go at all.

The little boy turned to the first giant. "Bend down," he said. The giant leaned down and the little boy whispered into his ear.

When the giant heard the secret, he leaped up from the table. His knees shook. His tongue hung out. "Oh, no!" he shouted. "That's terrible!" And he dashed from the castle, ran deep into the woods, and climbed to the top of a tall tree. He didn't come down for three days.

The second giant scowled at the little boy.

"What's wrong with him?" he asked.

"Never mind," said the little boy. "Just bend down."

The giant leaned down and the little boy stood on tiptoe and whispered into his ear.

When the giant heard the secret, he leaped up so fast that he knocked his chair over. His eyes rolled. His ears twitched. "Let me get away," he roared. And he raced from the castle, ran over the hills and crawled into the deepest, darkest cave he could find.

The third giant frowned down at the little boy.

"What's wrong with them?" he asked.

"Never mind," said the little boy. "Just bend down."

The giant leaned down and the little boy climbed on to a teacup and whispered into his ear.

When the giant heard the secret, he jumped up so fast that he ripped the seat of his trousers. His teeth chattered. His hair stood on end. "Help!" he cried. "Help!" And he dashed from the castle and dived head first into the muddy river.

The castle door had been left open, and since the giants had promised the little boy that he could go, he walked out and went home.

At last he was able to tell his mother his secret; but she didn't yell and run away. She just put him to bed and gave him some supper.

The next morning when the little boy woke up, he was covered from head to toe with bright red spots.

"Now I can tell *everybody* what my secret was," he said with a smile. "My secret was .... I'M GETTING THE MEASLES!"

Sunday Boots and Working Boots

Annette Penny

In a cupboard under the stairs of a little cottage lived two pairs of boots. Their names were Sunday Boots and Working Boots. They belonged to a man called Dad.

"Missus," he said to his wife on Sunday mornings, "have you seen my Sunday boots?"

"Yes, Dad," Missus answered. "They're under the stairs all cleaned and polished, ready to wear to church."

On hearing this Sunday Boots gleamed wickedly in the dim light of the cupboard.

"See, you dirty old working boots," they said. "We are off to church. Only the best boots are worn to church. You will never be worn to church. You are much too old and dirty!"

Sunday Boots, although smart and shiny, were not nice at all. In fact they were very nasty, particularly to Working Boots.

Dad was a farmer, and he wore Working Boots whilst he worked in the fields from Mondays to Saturdays. The fields were muddy, and the mud stuck to Working Boots. This happened so often that Dad said to Missus, "It's not worth cleaning my old working boots because they will only get covered in mud again tomorrow."

So Working Boots got dirtier and dirtier, muddier and muddier, and Sunday Boots hissed, "Get away from us, you filthy boots! We don't want you spoiling our shiny black polish! We can't understand why Dad puts you in the cupboard with us."

"We're sorry," said Working Boots sadly, "but we can't help being muddy."

Sunday Boots stuck their tongues out at Working Boots and said rudely, "Be quiet. We are going to sing.

We are going to sing one of the beautiful songs we hear when we are in church."

And they sang *All Things Bright and Beautiful.*

"That was lovely, Sunday Boots," said Working Boots. "You do sing well."

"Of course," Sunday Boots said grandly. "But then we are of the very best leather. We doubt if dirty things like you can sing, even if you know any songs."

"Oh, we know one song," said Working Boots eagerly. "Dad sings it when we are out in the fields. It goes like this."

They began to sing sweetly *My Old Man's a Dustman.*

"Stop! Stop!" shrieked Sunday Boots. "What a dreadfully common song, and what dreadfully common voices!"

They turned on their heels and settled themselves in the corner of the cupboard as far away from Working Boots as they could get.

One day, as Dad was pulling on Working Boots ready

for work, Missus said, "Dad, those old boots of yours are quite worn out. You'll have to buy some more."

Dad nodded his head. "Yes, you're right, Missus. There are two great holes in them that are quite past mending."

Working Boots were horrified.

"Whatever is going to happen to us?" they whispered fearfully to Sunday Boots when they were put away for the night.

"Why, don't you know?" sneered Sunday Boots. "You won't be needed any more. You'll be thrown away and you'll be able to sing *My Old Man's a Dustman* all the way to the dump where they put all the rest of the rubbish."

Working Boots felt sad and frightened. They did not feel any happier when, next day, Dad took Sunday Boots out of the cupboard and, although it was not yet Sunday, put them on to wear to the shops. All day long Working Boots stood by themselves in the cupboard.

"Oh dear," they sighed, "we really don't want to be thrown onto the rubbish dump. We like it here, even if Sunday Boots are horrible to us."

Great tears fell from their lace holes.

When Dad and Missus came home, Dad placed a brand new pair of boots in the cupboard. He picked up Working Boots and took them into the backyard. He was just about to throw them into the dustbin when he said, "You know, Missus, these old boots have been very good to me all these years. It seems a shame to throw them away." Suddenly, he smiled and said, "I don't think I will throw them away. I've an idea."

Dad carried Working Boots to his workshed and closed the door behind him.

Some time later, Dad came into the kitchen and beamed at Missus. He held out Working Boots. They were no longer dirty, but sparkling clean. Dad had brushed them thoroughly and given them a good coating of varnish. And in them he had planted two beautiful geraniums.

"My, my," Missus said in delight, "those boots make lovely plant pots. They will look just right on my kitchen window-sill."

Working Boots were overjoyed. From that day onwards they sat on the sill proudly holding their geraniums.

And what did Dad wear now when he went out to work in the fields?

Well, of course he did not want to spoil his smart new boots. So he wore Sunday Boots for work from Monday to Saturday. And soon they became muddy. Very muddy indeed.

BECAUSE OF FIGS

Ann Cameron

In the summer I like to lie in the grass and look at clouds and eat figs. Figs are soft and purple and delicious. Their juice runs all over my face, and I eat them till I'm so full I can't eat any more.

Because of figs I got a strange birthday present, and because of that birthday present I had some trouble. This is what happened.

It all started a long time ago when I had my fourth birthday. My father came home from work and said, "I have something for you, Julian! Go and look in the car."

I ran to look, and Huey ran after me, tripping on his shoelaces.

When we looked on the back seat of the car, there was a tree! A small tree with just a few leaves.

We ran back to my father. "A tree for a birthday present!" I said.

"A tree for a birthday present!" Huey said. He was two years old,

34

and he always repeated everything I said.

"It's a fig tree," my father told me. "It will grow as fast as you grow, Julian, and in a few years it will have figs that you can pick and eat."

I could hardly wait to grow my own sweet juicy purple figs. We planted the tree by our back fence, and I gave it water every day. And then one morning it had two new leaves.

"Fig tree, you're growing!" I said. I thought I should be growing

too. There is a mark on the wall in the bathroom of our house, where my father measures us, and I ran into the house to measure myself against my old mark. I pressed my hand against my head, flat to the wall, and checked where my hand was compared to the old mark. I wasn't any taller.

I walked outside to the fig tree. "I'm not any taller," I said. I touched the fig tree's new leaves. "I want to grow, too!" I said. "You know how to grow, and I don't!" I told the fig tree.

The fig tree didn't say a word.

"Maybe what makes you grow will make me grow," I told it. And very quickly, I picked the fig tree's new leaves and ate them. They tasted worse than spinach. I was pretty sure they would make me grow.

I did a little growing dance around the fig tree, with my hands raised high in the air.

It worked. I stayed taller than Huey. I got taller than my fig tree. And every time my fig tree got new leaves, I saw them and ate them secretly. And when nobody was looking, I did a growing dance.

"If you don't like this, fig tree, just tell me," I'd say.

The fig tree never said a word.

After a year my father looked at my fig tree. "It's a nice little tree," he said, "but it isn't growing." And he started putting fertilizer on my tree, and he looked at it more often.

But when new leaves showed, I saw them first. And I wanted to get taller, so I ate them.

Another whole year went by.

My mark on the bathroom wall went up three inches. I was four inches taller than Huey, and my arm muscle was twice as big as his.

The fig tree hadn't grown at all.

"Fig tree," I said, when I took its new leaves, "I'm sorry, but I want to grow tall."

And the fig tree didn't say a word.

One day my father was in the garden. He walked over to my fig tree. "Julian," he said, "something is the matter with your tree. It hasn't grown. It hasn't grown at all."

"Really?" I said. I didn't look at my father. I didn't look at my fig tree either.

"Do you have any idea what could be wrong?" my father asked.

I looked straight at my feet. I crossed my toes inside my shoes.

"Oh, no."

"I think that tree's just plain no good. We'll pull it out of the ground and get another one."

"Oh no! Don't do that!" I begged.

"Julian," my father said, "do you know something about this tree that I don't know?"

I didn't say anything. And I was glad, very glad, that the fig tree didn't say a word. Finally I said, "It's my tree. Give it one more chance."

"No use waiting around!" my father said. His hand was around the trunk of my tree.

"Please!" I said.

My father's hand relaxed. "After all, it *is* your tree," he said. "Just tell me when you want another one."

All afternoon I couldn't think of anything but all the little fig leaves I'd eaten. I was pretty sure I knew why the fig tree didn't grow.

At bedtime I couldn't sleep, and when Huey went to sleep, I got up and sneaked outside to my fig tree. I told God I knew that the fig leaves belonged to the fig tree. I told the fig tree I was sorry, and I promised I would never eat its leaves again.

The fig tree didn't say a word – but the next week it
got two new leaves, and kept them. That night I went to
bed happy, and I dreamed a good dream. My fig tree was
higher than the house, I was almost as tall as my dad, and
there were big figs, juicy figs, sweet figs, falling all over
the lawn.